IR

DISCARD

SAM THE ZAMBONI MAN

BY JAMES STEVENSON

ILLUSTRATED BY HARVEY STEVENSON

GREENWILLOW BOOKS, NEW YORK

Library of Congress Cataloging-in-Publication Data

Stevenson, James, (date)
Sam the Zamboni man / by James Stevenson ;
pictures by Harvey Stevenson.
    p.   cm.
Summary: Matt visits his grandfather, who
operates the Zamboni at the hockey rink,
and on his last night there, he becomes
the youngest Zamboni driver of all time.
ISBN 0-688-14484-5 (trade).
ISBN 0-688-14485-3 (lib. bdg.)
[1. Grandfathers—Fiction.
2. Zambonis (Trademark)—Fiction.
3. Skating rinks—Fiction. 4. Hockey—Fiction.]
I. Stevenson, Harvey, (date) ill.   II. Title.
PZ7.S84748Sam   1998   [E]—dc21
97-6946   CIP   AC

For Alex
—H. S.

1

Matt lived in the country. He'd seen kids play hockey on the pond behind his school, but he'd never been to a real hockey game in the city.

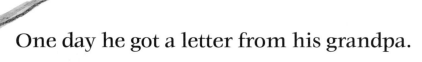

One day he got a letter from his grandpa.

"Come to the city for a visit, Matt," said the letter,
"and we'll go to a hockey game together."

Matt's grandpa worked at a huge stadium. He drove
the Zamboni—the big blue-and-white machine that
rolled around the rink, melting and scraping and
smoothing the ice.

People called him Sam the Zamboni Man.

"Can I go to Grandpa's?" Matt asked his parents.

"I want to see a hockey game and watch Grandpa
drive the Zamboni."

His parents said yes.

2

Matt's grandpa took him to a hockey game on the first night of his visit. They went into the stadium and bought a box of Cracker Jack to share. There was a big crowd, but their seats were very close to the rink, and Matt could see everything that happened.

A friend of Grandpa's had cleared the ice, so it was glistening when the game began.

Matt loved watching the players in bright uniforms zoom by at top speed, chasing the small black puck. He loved the sound of skates scraping, and hockey sticks clattering and smacking, and the way the crowd yelled and cheered and jumped to its feet.

Near the end of the first period Matt's grandpa said, "I have to go to work now. Will you sit right here and wait until I come back?"

"Sure, Grandpa," said Matt.

A few minutes later a loud buzzer sounded, and the hockey teams skated off the ice. It was the end of the first period.

Music began to play over the loudspeaker. Then, from the far end of the rink, the blue-and-white Zamboni came rolling slowly out onto the ice. Matt's grandpa was at the wheel.

When his grandpa went by, Matt waved. His grandpa waved back. Matt felt very proud. He felt as if all the people in the stadium knew that Sam was his grandpa.

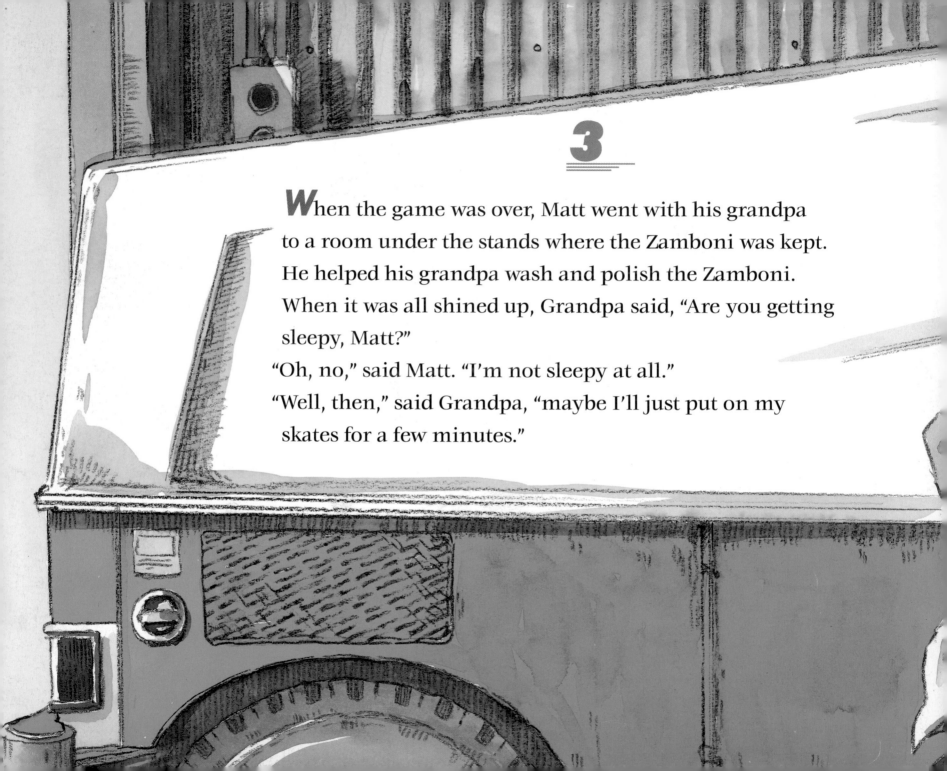

3

When the game was over, Matt went with his grandpa
to a room under the stands where the Zamboni was kept.
He helped his grandpa wash and polish the Zamboni.
When it was all shined up, Grandpa said, "Are you getting
sleepy, Matt?"

"Oh, no," said Matt. "I'm not sleepy at all."

"Well, then," said Grandpa, "maybe I'll just put on my
skates for a few minutes."

Grandpa went to a battered green locker and took out
an old pair of hockey skates. The laces had been broken
so many times they were mostly knots. But Grandpa
put the skates on and tied them up.
From the back of the locker he took a splintery
hockey stick that was bandaged with black tape.

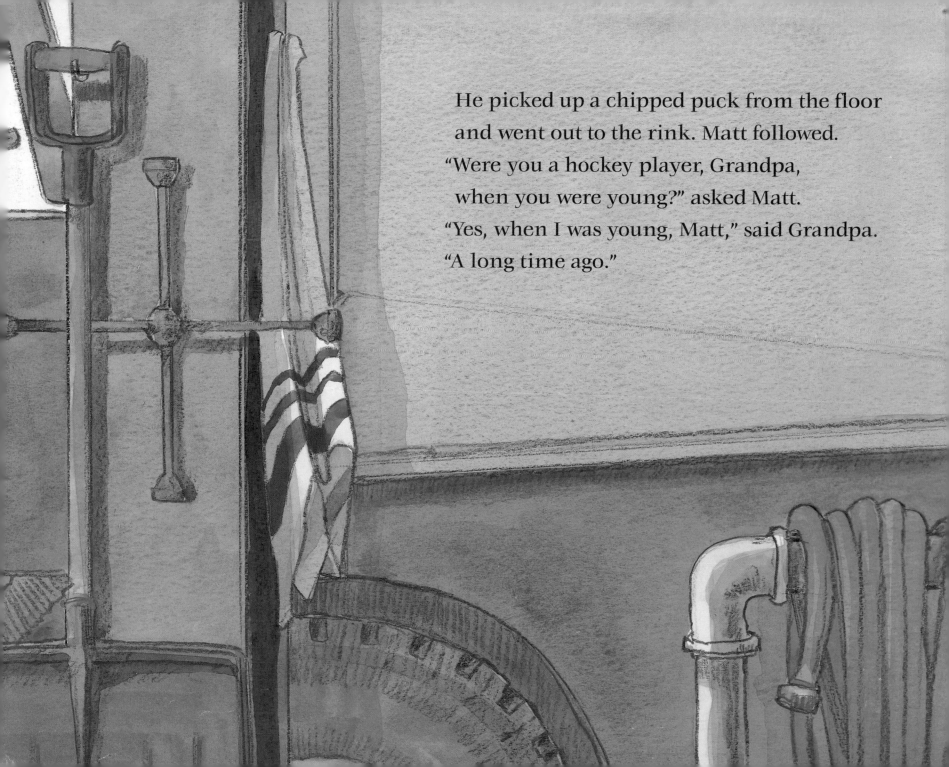

He picked up a chipped puck from the floor
and went out to the rink. Matt followed.
"Were you a hockey player, Grandpa,
when you were young?" asked Matt.
"Yes, when I was young, Matt," said Grandpa.
"A long time ago."

The stadium was dark now. There was only a single light
hanging over the rink. Matt watched as his grandpa glided
out onto the ice and began to skate, steering the puck ahead
of him.

Grandpa's shadow made long shapes as he sailed around the
rink. The only sound was the scratching of skate blades.
Back and forth Grandpa skated, the puck always ahead of him.
Suddenly he stopped, sending a shower of ice into the air.
Then he started again, skating faster and faster toward the goal.
He drew back his stick. *WHACK!* The puck flew into the net.

Matt clapped and cheered. His grandpa raised his stick in the air and waved to Matt, grinning. Then he turned and waved to the rows and rows of empty seats.

"Who were you waving to, Grandpa?" asked Matt.

"Oh, I thought maybe I heard some cheering," said Grandpa. "Guess I was wrong." He laughcd.

"I was cheering," said Matt.

"I *know* you were," said Grandpa, and he gave Matt a hug.

4

On the last night of Matt's visit Grandpa asked,
"Would you like to go to the stadium again tonight?"
"Can we?" said Matt. "I'd really like that."
But when they got there, the stadium was closed.
"I guess there isn't any game tonight," said Matt.
He was really disappointed, but he didn't want
his grandpa to know.

"It doesn't matter,
Grandpa," he said.
"I've had lots of fun."
"So have I, Matt," said his grandpa. "Let's go in,
anyway." He took a key out of his pocket and
unlocked a side door.
They stood looking down over the dark, empty seats.
The stadium was very still and gloomy looking.
"Let's go home, Grandpa," said Matt.
"Wait here just a minute," said Grandpa.
Matt waited while his grandpa ran down the stairs
and disappeared.

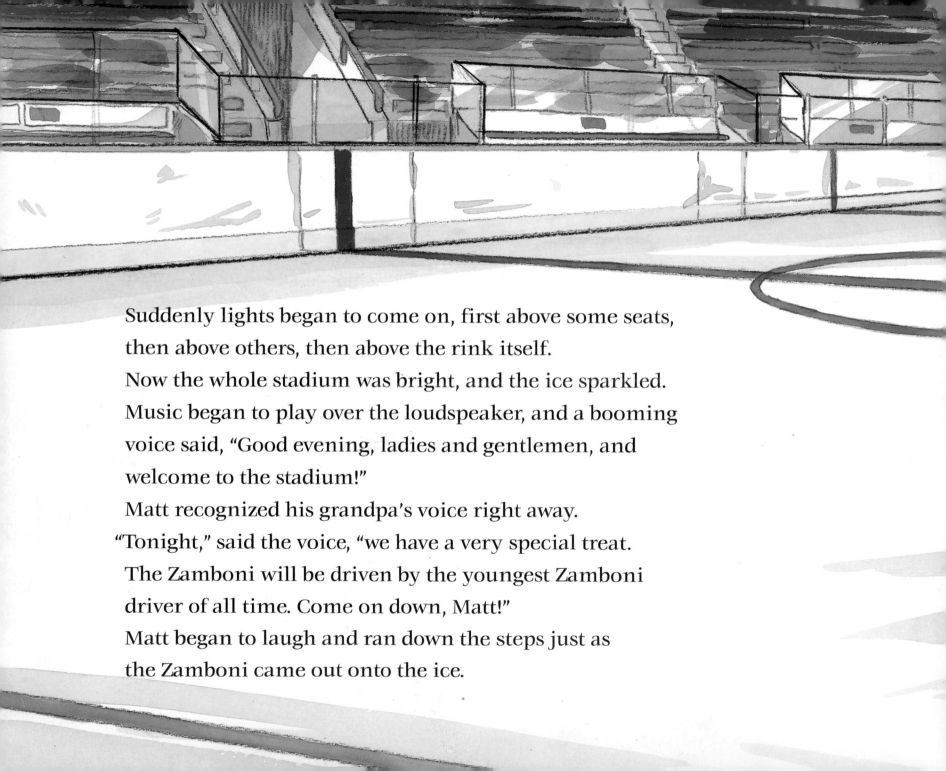

Suddenly lights began to come on, first above some seats, then above others, then above the rink itself.

Now the whole stadium was bright, and the ice sparkled.

Music began to play over the loudspeaker, and a booming voice said, "Good evening, ladies and gentlemen, and welcome to the stadium!"

Matt recognized his grandpa's voice right away.

"Tonight," said the voice, "we have a very special treat. The Zamboni will be driven by the youngest Zamboni driver of all time. Come on down, Matt!"

Matt began to laugh and ran down the steps just as the Zamboni came out onto the ice.

His grandpa got down and lifted Matt
onto the Zamboni. Then he climbed
back on and sat Matt on his lap.
Matt held the wheel. He felt very high
in the air, looking down on the rink.
It was almost scary.
"Ready to roll, Matt?" said his grandpa.
"What do I do, Grandpa?" asked Matt.
There were a lot of levers and gearshifts.
"Just steer, that's all," said his grandpa,
and the Zamboni began to roll forward.
"Here we go!"

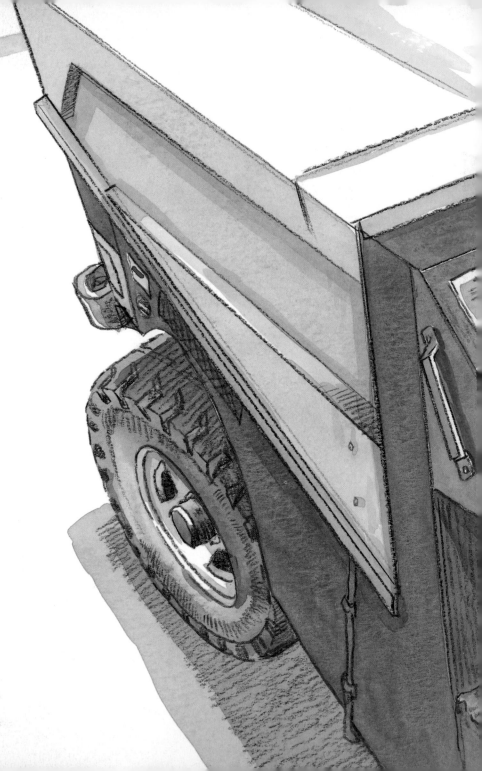

Matt held the wheel steady. After a while he tried
turning it a little bit to the right. The Zamboni
went to the right. He turned the wheel to the left.
The Zamboni swung to the left.

Matt steered the Zamboni in a big loop.

And another big loop.

Then a figure eight.

Then a zigzag back.

Matt was laughing now, and so was his
grandpa. It was the most fun Matt had
ever had. He covered the ice with circles
and swirls and loops.

He tried to write a gigantic *G* for *Grandpa*.
It didn't look perfect, but then he wrote an *M*
for *Matt*, and that one was pretty good.

Matt ended by zigzagging all the way down the entire rink.

Then he steered the Zamboni carefully out the gate and back to its room under the stands.

"That was great, Grandpa," said Matt on the way home. "Can we
do it again next year if I come to visit?"

"I think we may be too busy to spend time driving the Zamboni,"
said Grandpa.

"Why?" said Matt.

"Because next year, when you come to visit, I'll be teaching you
how to skate and how to play hockey. Would you like that, Matt?"

"Yes, I would," said Matt. "A *lot*."

"So would I," said Grandpa, and they both laughed.